MRS. OWL
AND
MR. PIG

by JAN WAHL

illustrated by EILEEN CHRISTELOW

Dutton   Lodestar Books   New York

Library of Congress Cataloging-in-Publication Data

Wahl, Jan.

Mrs. Owl and Mr. Pig / by Jan Wahl: illustrated by Eileen
Christelow. — 1st ed.

p. cm.

Summary: A lonely widow in need of money, Mrs. Owl advertises for a
boarder, but her new lodger, Mr. Pig, seems to be more trouble than he's worth.

ISBN 0-525-67311-3

[1. Pigs—Fiction. 2. Owls—Fiction.] I. Christelow, Eileen, ill.
II. Title.

PZ7.W1266MR 1991

[E] — dc20

89-13428 CIP AC

Published in the United States by Lodestar Books,
an affiliate of Dutton Children's Books,
a division of Penguin Books USA Inc.

Published simultaneously in Canada by
McClelland & Stewart, Toronto

Editor: Virginia Buckley   Designer: Marilyn Granald, LMD

Printed in Hong Kong
First Edition   10 9 8 7 6 5 4 3 2 1

to Brer Stu
and Sis Miriam
J.W.

Mrs. Owl was a widow.

She was tired of living alone in an empty, silent cottage. One morning, she counted her pennies. Three were left. She made up her mind.

"This house is spooky. I need somebody to share things with!"

She looked at the picture of Hector Owl over the fireplace.

"He was wise. But . . . he is gone."

So, on the front door she hung a sign. It said:

ROOM & BOARD
REASONABLE RATES
ASK WITHIN—
    LOUELLA OWL,
    PROPRIETOR
PLEASE WIPE FEET!

The cottage had gotten dusty. She swept the floor
and polished everything in sight. Mr. Owl used
to help with the dusting.

She wiped off the grandfather clock that had
stopped ticking. How she loved that clock!

At last, Mrs. Owl knew everything looked gleaming
and perfect.

Soon came a knock at the door. A stout gentleman
wearing a hat and tie wiped his feet.
"Hi. I'll take the room. My name is George Pig."
"One dollar each week, everything included," said
Mrs. Owl. They shook hoof and wing.

Mr. Pig took off his hat and tie, and sat down at the table in the kitchen.

Mrs. Owl collected her dollar from him and dashed over to Mole's Delicatessen. When she returned, she made a beautiful omelet.

Mr. Pig gobbled it down. "Not bad for a start!" he oinked.

He yawned. "Guess I'll take a nap." And Mr. Pig fell asleep right at the table.

"I was hoping we could have a conversation," said Mrs. Owl. She tiptoed out the door.

She flew up into the elm tree to think. "Anyway, I'm not alone now." She sighed.

Soon smoke poured out of the tin chimney.

Mr. Pig shouted from the window, "Hi, there's no butter."

Muttering to herself, Mrs. Owl went back to Mole's Delicatessen. When she returned, the cottage was wing-high in popcorn. Mr. Pig was tossing salt around. He didn't offer Mrs. Owl even a little bowl.

After he finished eating, he said, "Guess I'll take a nap." And he flopped down on the rug.

Mrs. Owl stepped around Mr. Pig.

She took two cups and invited her neighbor, Abigail Chipmunk, to the elm for afternoon tea.

"What shall I *do?*" grumbled Mrs. Owl. "Silly pig."

"Be very wise," said Abigail Chipmunk. "Give Mr. Pig a list of Do's and Don'ts."

Luckily, Mrs. Owl had a pen. She pulled leaves off the elm and began to write some rules.

She had a good pile of them, when suddenly Abigail Chipmunk cried, "Look! Look at that!"

There was Mr. Pig, moving boxes of different sizes into Mrs. Owl's little cottage.

Hurrying home, she found him setting up lots of woodworking equipment.

"My hobby," he oinked. Mrs. Owl pushed the pile of leaves with Do's and Don'ts at him.

"Read!" she hooted angrily and stood in front of him.

"Doesn't say here I can't have a hobby," he grunted. "Says . . . um, I must ask you for the salt. Can't nap on the floor. I must stay in my room unless I am invited. And use the kitchen only if I have company."

He took off his glasses, bowing. Grimly Mrs. Owl stuck the leaves up everywhere.

Mr. Pig kept opening up boxes. He moved
everything into his room. He began to make such
a racket! Hour after hour his saw buzzed. Sawdust
flew out of his room.

Mrs. Owl rushed up the elm to write more Do's and Don'ts.

"It's not fun to live alone," she said. "However, Mr. Pig is something else."

She whistled a tune to keep her spirits from sinking. Along came her neighbor, Abigail Chipmunk.

"Hello, Mrs. Owl. How are things with you and Mr. Pig?"

HAMMER! HAMMER!

BANG! BANG!

"My goodness," said the chipmunk. "What is he doing?"

Feathers in a flap, Mrs. Owl flew. Her neighbor darted below. Together, they looked in the window.

Mr. Pig was making lopsided stools.

"Stop that!" shouted Mrs. Owl.

"I asked guests for supper," Mr. Pig oinked. "But you don't have enough chairs!"

"Or food," said Mrs. Owl.

"We bring our own," Mr. Pig sniffed proudly.

That evening, when Mrs. Owl opened the door, six
pigs trooped in wearing chef's hats. They wiped their
feet on the mat and tramped through to the kitchen.

They cooked lots of spaghetti . . .

Sauce dripped in great big puddles. Water bubbled over. Globs of steam clouded the place!

Mrs. Owl sat alone, staring at the painting of Hector Owl.

All at once Mr. Pig stood there, his head bowed. "Here is a plate of spaghetti," he moaned. "What is wrong with it?"

Slowly, she tried it.

Mrs. Owl gagged. "Yuck! But it won't be hard to make it taste better."

Mr. Pig followed her from the parlor to the garden.
She picked some basil, some parsley and oregano.
In the busy kitchen, she stirred these into the sauce.
A pinch of sugar, too.

"Yum," said the six pigs.

"Yum," burped Mr. Pig.

The kitchen was a mess.

"Mr. Pig," said Mrs. Owl, "clean this up." With that, she fled to her room.

She banged the door shut, which rattled the
grandfather clock in the hall.

"The clock has stopped and so has my life," she
sobbed. Mrs. Owl pulled thick covers over her head.

After a while, she heard funny sounds and
peeked out.

All the pig guests had left.

But . . .

Coils and springs and screws lay scattered all over the floor.

Mr. Pig had taken the clock apart. Mrs. Owl shook her wing at him. "Mr. Pig, you are impossible. In the morning, you must go! You are good for nothing!"

"I was trying to fix it," Mr. Pig oinked woefully.

All night long, Mrs. Owl heard *pings* and *pangs* and other odd noises from the hall.

"He must be packing his bags," she said. She buried her head under the pillow.

In the morning, a pink-yellow sun rose. Mrs. Owl
was awakened by a special sound.
    BONG BONG BONG BONG BONG BONG
BONG! Seven bongs.

She put on her best dress. "Mr. Pig," she declared, over a hot, tasty stack of blueberry pancakes, "you are good for *something*. You fixed my clock."

"Thanks." He yawned. He had stayed up all night.

"We can go into business together," Mrs. Owl said. "I will cook. You will fix clocks."

Mr. Pig oinked, "I can stay?"

"Silly pig!"

Soon a new sign hung at the door:

TUMMIES FED
& CLOCKS FIXED
ASK WITHIN—
OWL & PIG,
PROPRIETORS
PLEASE WIPE FEET!